YEE: THE NOVEL

BY MICHAEL SEAN DILLON

ZIPPOBEAST PRODUCTIONS
Venice Beach, California

YEE: The Novel

BY MICHAEL SEAN DILLON

Dedicated to a wonderful brother

Whom I loved while he was living and whom I love while

He's dead.

Woody Hugoboom. September 26 1970-November 7 1989.

Woody, I love you!

And to the Infinite Allness.

And now to Lolita.

"At the appointed hour you shall come to the heart of all-though at what hour the gates shall open on to fairer fields no mortal ever knows" : IX interpretation of Bhagavad Gita

The New Gita by W.L. Violette

"Why would fear want to oppose truth?
Because truth has the power to
transform fear.
Fear believes it is fighting for its life":

Emmanuel's Book.

"In the jungle of civilization, in the stress
Of modern living lies the test.
Whatever you give out will come back to you…
When you fill yourself with inharmonious thoughts
And emotions, you are destroying yourself. Why hate
Or be angry with anyone? Love your enemies.":

Paramahansa Yogananda in Man's Eternal Quest

"On behalf of myself and the rest of your
Subconscious anxieties, we thought you should
be given advance notice regarding our plan
to jump out and grab you this evening." :

Berke Breathed in <u>Toons for Our Times.</u>

It began when I woke and looked in the mirror. I was there again, and as usual I wanted to cry at the sight of my own face. My dark hair and green eyes, my face men say is so pretty, my breasts which cling to the very existence of my dress, my lips which want nothing more than to whisper intimacies to the man who treats me like a stranger, all of me I saw put disgust in my head. So I slammed the mirror and walked out into the world. My name is Susan Pikkins and I work in the city at a financing company.

I exist not- but I shall born myself as you read. You are my creator- my god- and my servant. It is nice to be someone powerless- yet with power. Each word you read of me- the more you make me- and I have nothing to do with you. Read on! Ah- I am stretching my arms- yes- let me scratch my back.

You know the story of me by now. How you were told who I am by that acquaintance of yours. How you weren't sure whether he was a reliable source of information, but by drawing some median you were able to siphon the true from the embellished.

You of course learned that I am a mechanic- though I do not like working on Fords, they; nonetheless, are my specialty. I am the mechanic who has read about your work. I picked up a magazine while in the shitter in Alabama and fate made the page display your article- or at least the one you've always wanted to write. I am happy to make your acquaintance. You know my name, and how could I not know yours. Everyone knows you- or at least those of substance.

It is amazing how I stumbled upon your piece. It influenced me profoundly. It brought a whole new dimension to my understanding of the world. Sort of like what that guy Jung says happens with people is like what happens with chemicals. Your article changed me- just like my words are changing you- I am being created.

*:*This is what Joe Simpson read in a pamphlet of college writing pieces which sat on the table in the café he occupied.

The day went normally at first. I caught the right bus. It carried me to the right place, and in the wake of rightness I strolled into the right building and began the routine of a day, full of rightness and all that goes along with the ordinary.

The clock ticked and let all life around it know the time, which no one questioned- which no one ceased to worship. As the big hand came upon the 2, a realization conquered my head. The second hand swirled like a monster of power around the dial of roundness. The life around me continued its rightness, doing all the ordinary things of the job. As that big hand came to the 2 I realized I was no longer a human. I had transformed.

Joe Simpson continued to read:

Do you know it was just after supper on the fifth of May, that I realized the whole story about the world was wrong. The fact missing in God's story has to do with me. I was not accounted for in God's creation. The first word was light; others followed- but he made no mention of me. What am I to think? It seems reality can not exist without me- just as I can't exist without you; and, dear friend, you can not exist without me!

Anyway, God did forget us. Though I am not saying it was not on purpose. I suppose he can include us when he wants to, and you know friend- he is going to when I am through and you are through reading what I have written. You must excuse me. I have to go- I've an engagement- a coffee date- I'll be seeing you later.

To Joe Simpson's surprise a human figure climbed out of the pamphlet on the table, as if it were some portal. First his head appeared, then his torso and finally the legs. He pulled himself onto the table and brushed off some dust. Joe looked all about the café to see if anyone else saw what was happening. No one else seemed to register it as "reality". The man on the table talked to Joe Simpson then stepped down and walked out the door.

And so out of the room walked Bolovo Pete. The room which he left still existed and, to this day it still exists. In the small city of Santa Cruz in the American province of California, the first meeting between Joe Simpson and Bolovo Pete took place. You have just witnessed it. I must catch you up on what occurred before this meeting.

But on the other hand,

It was Tuesday at three o'clock and Susan Pikkins was locked inside the bathroom of the office where she worked howling like a pregnant sow. Her fellow workers were gathered around the locked door listening in amazement.

"Susan, stop playing. The jokes over- what are you doing?"

"WEEEEEEE! WEEEE! WEEEEEE!!"

"Susan, what are you doing?"

"She's acting like a pig or something-"

"Is she joking?"

"Is it April?-"

"What the hell's all the noise- who?"

"WEEEEE! WEEEEEEEE! WEEE! WEEE!"

The boss was Glen Smackins and he was told of the disturbance over the phone so he got into his Mercedes and drove to his building. The crowd bothered him.

"Get back to work- Scat!! I'll take care of this. Who's got the keys?"

"Jenkins" was the answer.

"Get me Jenkins. Get back to work, everybody- give me those keys. Thanks- You go back to work too."

They all went back to their desks with their full attention on the door. Glen Smackins opened the door and found Susan Pikkins squatting in the corner naked on all fours squealing like a pig.

Joe had entered the café to take some coffee and some nicotine and some relaxation. He had arrived with the plan to attend a movie, but as plans can change with the introduction of some outside anything- Joe decided not to go to the movie after he witnesses the form of Bolovo Pete.

To say it straightforward and in a nutshell- Bolovo Pete greatly disturbed Joe Simpson. The very existence of this "disturbing manifestation" ruptured Joe's serenity. He received feelings of disgust by the other's presence, and when it seemed Bolovo Pete began addressing him as "You" and "My friend", Joe slowly moved away from the table and the pamphlet from which Bolovo Pete emerged- but of course, this didn't work.

Bolovo Pete was persistent and a lost gaze of familiarity shone from his eyes. I can not say whether he could have known of Joe Simpson's article or not, though I assume he couldn't have for it had not yet been published and was due to come out in the next issue of The Coastal Cruz. Joe Simpson was disturbed because this "dreadful stranger", who had just stepped out of a sheet of paper, knew who he was, and that he had written an article. He felt a horror familiar to those who feel that they've been watched in the past, when such never before seemed possible.

I became a pig. It just happened when that long hand hit the two. The rightness became wrong and all those people working around me vanished. I was in a stable of mud. Creamy dark mud of blackness. The clock disappeared.

The purpose of life which had been to approve of some meaningless scribble, and seek sexual intimacy, vanished. I was alone in happiness in a most amazing pool of mud. I ran into a corner and rolled in the cool substance. The feeling of relief from the cold mud I can not relate. A hot body in icy mud. I was filled with supreme satisfaction- beyond the weak foreplay and detached sexuality of my past.

This bliss persisted until some strange animal walked up to me and would not go away. It just gazed and made some sort of sound. It appeared harmless so I ignored it and continued to roll in the mud.

Soon more of these animals gathered around me next to the first one. I became cornered and a sudden fright filled me. A frantic impulse. A fear of them. A fear of the potential. I ran. Broke through the wall of their legs. Ran as fast as mine would move. Down the stairs. Through a wall space and into the city street.

Joe walked to the counter and ordered a beer. He didn't drink often, but after what had just happened, in this mind puddle he'd stepped into, he felt a beer was a good thing.

With the lager he sat at the table and sipped, watching a picture on the wall. The picture had nothing to do with him except that it shared the same spot in time and space- and in a matter shall we say- as him. At this moment the picture- which was of a cat walking alone on a small planet- became the center of the universe. He became that cat walking on a small planet. The cat became Joe Simpson, and the artist of the painting was in another part of Santa Cruz going down on his blonde haired girlfriend- which has nothing to do with the plot of this story.

It was three thirty and Susan Pikkins was naked on all fours in the street of the city. She ran along on all fours while pedestrians stopped in disbelief and watched her body slide by. Her fellow workers looked out from their windows. Several even chased her outside, but unable to catch her, they ran back up the steps and fumbled over the phone trying to call the police.

"Officer, one of our workers is out on the street naked running around on all fours. No! This isn't a joke! - You have to believe me- See I told you! You're gonna get a million calls- her name? She's really a good employee. This is the strangest- Susan- Susan Pikkins- Yes. Here? -This is Top Financial on Broadway- she just darted out the door- we found her in the bathroom squealing like a pig- She just ran past us we couldn't catch her!..."

Glen Smackins made the phone call, and while he was talking to the police lady, Susan continued her flight down the street. He was upset his workers hadn't given him the opportunity to be alone with their naked kneeling office beauty. The pain of potentiality yanked his loins.

As I was telling you before, my friend, we've got nothing in common and everything in common. You eat and drink while I do not- But bother not to think much of this- I am alive and becoming more and more so as you read- So read- Read on, my fine friend.

How I do enjoy your company. You are one to be reckoned with- You are the type to write an article which could change the life of someone like me. You must listen to me some more, dear friend. You need me as much as I you.

Joe Simpson could no longer endure this second meeting with the "madman" Bolovo Pete. The other night at the café had rattled his nerves; this time, at the bus station, was too much.

He had picked up the newspaper to read, and he was face to face with the above in fine black newsprint. He tried to stop reading, but couldn't until he'd glanced through every word. Then Bolovo Pete appeared before him. And as usual, no one else seemed to see him.

Joe stood up and stared at the sitting figure, which wore a beat leather jacket and held a cigarette between its fingers. He looked into "the madman's" eyes- and shook his head, then walked off to find a new bus stop.

What finally happened has become the talk of town for several months now. It took us by surprise. It happened on some Tuesday in October- no one would argue it was Wednesday- but no matter the day, it was the event which put Santa Cruz on the world's recognitional map. What more can be said. You must see what is meant.

Susan Pikkins ran into a supermarket. The customers whispered and pointed and soon a crowd gathered around her. Down the aisles she ran sniffing the merchandise, gliding along on hands and knees.

The manager was notified and approached her. He was excited by her. It was like one of those centerfolds coming to life and crawling out of the magazine and down the aisle. Something of this sort was a recurring dream in his life, and as he saw this apparition of his fantasies crawling down the linoleum floors of his own supermarket, he choked up in the throat from nervousness and enticement.

"Excuse me ma'am. –Ma'am? - Someone call the police"

Someone called the police while Susan darted past the crouching manager, who was wide in the eyes and of a seedy heartbeat, past some women and awed children, down the produce lane and out the electric doors.

Hello Joe. I exist fully and completely now- You no longer need read me anymore. I don't need you- Oh I did friend- before I was just a nothing, but thanks to your effort- your patient effort- I've been made. I exist and now you can not do anything about it. I am solid, whole and complete- you think you don't care and this is ok, but it really doesn't matter, for you know how it is- friend or enemy, one a piece each is- But I'd like to thank you anyway-

Joe Simpson put down a box which he held in his lap as Bolovo Pete stood finishing these words. Joe had been waiting for such a visit. It was not a surprise for him to see Bolovo Pete in whole human form. He was not surprised that other humans could now see him. He was not surprised that he didn't have to read him to life first, that the above was delivered in audible sounds which everyone in the world could have heard.

He sat motionless at his table at the café, then spoke eight words with stoic simplicity:

"You do not exist and you never will."

Then he pulled the lid off the box in his lap and turned the bottom of the open structure toward the standing figure.

A mighty shriek-   a yell and

Thunder-

Bolovo Pete began to fall into a puddle which evaporated into nothing. No clothes, no skin, no nothing was left. The earth shook fiercely and bricks of the café began to tumble. People screamed, and ran from the crumbling walls. This was the moment later known as the Great Quake from Santa Cruz. This trembling killed people at the café who had previously been reading, talking and drinking coffee, oblivious to the presence of Bolovo Pete and Joe Simpson.

Not only this café, but the whole Pacific Garden Mall and many houses were devastated- not to mention roads and overpasses which collapsed in San Francisco and in Oakland. The World Series was postponed and much of the bay area went black without power.

At the moment of its beginning, while the café walls fell around him, Joe Simpson bent over and looked into the bottom of the box, which held a simple mirror. He was face to face with his own image.

I was running past animals and things in a panic. Each turn brought me to more of them. They'd bend down and look at me with shocked eyes. "I am all I am" kept flying through my head. My knees were bleeding, my hands sore, the dirt on my stomach and breasts began to darken- still, on I ran- on and on to never stop till I came to tranquility. I could feel the oppression of desire from the eyes which saw me. I could feel their tongues licking, feel their hands stroking, all through the eyes- all through the eyes.

Joe Simpson, amidst the quaking rubble, watched in horror as his dissolved enemy transformed into earthly destruction. Walls collapsed to the soil, and terror filled the pressurized air while bricks rolled over white metal tables and abandoned books. Joe looked past the tables, beyond the caving walls and shrieking humans. He looked into the voidless- seeing fear and power.

Next he was running. Running away from the destruction and pain, but he could find nowhere to stop, nowhere to center himself. He kept running. He felt in motion like a pendulum spinning in circles. Like a circle of eternity which spins and spins; a top with no form; a dimensionless line. Eternity, alone.

I found tranquility once I got away from everything. No more staring creatures wanting to eat me. No more oppression. No more repulsion, and confusion. Alone, I was content. The mud appeared again. My mind went to wandering. I saw myself writing something like a note to the world; a note to those things who knew me; to those things I thought I cared about and to those I thought I didn't. I wrote something which I can only paraphrase as such, in my head, in a dark print:

"have you ever felt disconnected in some way but still there and observing and floating in the world- silence with seeing- outside looking in to where you yourself are- amidst humans- amidst yourself- yet not doing what you desire to be doing- waiting as time ticks- forgetting your alive- wondering what life is- wondering why we work and how all the things around you got there- wondering why we eat and dream and why things just happen and the connection between motivation and occurrences?

What is it all anyway? Have you ever wanted to talk and felt like there's no one to listen? Or like you are not allowing yourself to go to those who will listen? Have you ever understood how substances and busy-ness in life can be an escape from such thinking? Have you ever felt you're plummeting down some worldly toilet while in fact you know that this is not true- and things really are working for the better? Have you ever felt alone and in desire of understanding and appreciation and also warm holding- a beautiful opposite sexed partner's strength in holding and helping you? Have you ever wondered if you are the lamest person in the whole world in terms of talking- meeting other people- sharing? - growing?" Then it ended with a feeling of releaseful honesty which I can only paraphrase as:

"I have!!" The ending had depth which I couldn't understand. It was both discouraging and somehow helpful.

I was huddled in a drainage pipe under a cement road holding my naked knees against my dirty breasts, staring at the mud between my toes. I couldn't look to the right, nor to the left only at my toes. They and my body were caked with grime, like a layer of paint with sweat trails making horizontal roads along my stomach. I am slender and brunette, and was naked as a pig.

The great quake of Santa Cruz began as Bolovo Pete faced the mirror Joe Simpson held toward him. The image of nothing reflected from something cracked reality in its invisible center. The mountains of Nisene State Park split. The land everyone stood on lost equilibrium, and schedules made in peoples 'minds died, along with Bolovo Pete, the perceived apparition of potentiality, - at least in Joe Simpson's eyes.

The next morning Joe Simpson woke in his room in a strange mood. He looked around and saw the ordinary setting of his dwelling. The room was whole. A few things were broken. The bowl which used to keep the fish Timmy alive, some new plates and a mayonnaise jar were shattered. The fish was dead- or at least out of breath.

Joe remembered the results of his last experience with Bolovo Pete, then entered a state of panic. Rushing out the door, he saw people in front of their houses repairing chimneys, talking to neighbors, cleaning up glass. They were doing the unordinary. He stood for a moment and imagined, "Would none of this have happened if I didn't point the mirror at him?" He looked to the sun and went back into the house.

The highway was deserted, and grass grew in wet tufts along its side. One of those cement circular tunnels which carry water under the road came into Bolovo Pete's view as he strolled along the abandoned fields next to the city's road. He saw what appeared to be a figure in the tunnel.

After stopping and staring for a moment, he walked in that direction. It was a beautiful figure- that of a naked woman. Bolovo Pete walked to the tunnel's entrance and feasted his eyes on the filthy, long, unclothed and slender shape of a woman curled into a ball and shivering in light sleep.

He took off his leather coat and draped it around her. She snuggled around the leather warmth and drifted into a deeper slumber. Pulling a cigarette from his shirt pocket and puffing in the air, he sat and observed the fields around him as the woman slept.

I woke in a drainage pipe and there was an animal sitting next to the entrance. It sat as if it were content, and I felt no threat. Rather, I was intrigued by it. I crept out of the pipe and looked more closely. Its eyes were closed. I felt safe. Drawing closer, I saw it looked like me. It was a pig too. The only difference was it wore clothes. It had tried to clothe me too, for I woke with a jacket on my body.

I licked its neck and it woke with alarm which became acceptance. I wanted to make it naked and free like me. I undressed it then we grasped each other and rolled in the crispness of mud and goo.

I accepted firmness and it brandished me within like a wisp of fire as we rolled and rolled finally resting against the drainage pipe.

It held me and I let it, and even held it. We fell asleep-though I think it was awake for some time. I could feel its eyes blink and look at the sky.

Bolovo Pete was holding the woman of flesh Susan Pikkins. It was in the fields along the side of Mission Street in the devastated city of Santa Cruz. The earthquake was real. Joe Simpson was in his room waking up at the same time Bolovo Pete was waking up inside Susan Pikkin's arms.

Bolovo Pete remembered the night and the rolling. He remembered finding her in the pipe. He touched her now, as the sun grew brighter and as occasional cars moved by. She woke and drew back.

"I am Bolovo Pete" he spoke.

She stared at him.

"We made love last night" he continued.

She still stared at him. Weeds all around were littered with his clothes. She looked at the mess of fabric and at the sun, then back at Bolovo Pete who got up to dress.

"I've got to wear clothes- You should too!" He looked her naked form over.

"Do you want some?"

As he held out his shirt to her, she drew back even further.

"You don't want my clothes? You don't like it when I talk to you, oh well. But do you know I know who you are? - Well of course I do. Susan Pikkins, executive worker gone mad. Escapee- tired of sex and games and mindless working and wasting of life. I know who you are. I helped create you so you could help create me. Ah, yes- you are my helper to belonging. You are an instrument to my power. You are captivated by my presence, though you don't trust me. What's new? It seems you all don't like me, but something attracts you to me- my nonexistence makes you want to make me real. All I do is pretend and you do the rest. You give me meaning. Ah- it was a rough day yesterday, Susan. Someone tried to kill me, but I survived.

"It takes more than a mirror to kill ol' Bolovo Pete. Much more than a mirror. Ah- you probably wonder why I want to exist? Why would I want to exist when you yourself- living flesh and all- don't want to? Why would I bother the living so that they conjure me to have form?

"It is to be what potentiality makes. If you didn't fear me I'd have no existence. If you didn't resist me I'd have no form- but, ah, you let my being come to life merely by giving me attention- by dwelling on what you don't like rather than on what you do like. I am the manifestation of your thoughts- of yours and many others! I could have been nice- but Susan, you made me this way. Anyway- love me or hate me, I must be going. I revoke the offer to my clothes. I need the shirt. Goodbye."

Bolovo Pete finished dressing and walked off along Mission toward the town. Susan watched him leave and gazed in amazement. She had not moved during his speech. Now she looked at a weed in front of her feet and tears trickled from her eyes. She clenched her bare knees and shivered from the briskness of morning air.

Bolovo Pete was a distant figure, trudging his way along the roadside. Susan Pikkins continued to cry and began to escape in a world of dreams.

Joe Simpson sat on his bed oblivious to the rest of the world. He thought only of the crumbling bricks and the haunting Bolovo Pete. He thought of the box with the mirror and of the earthquake everyone was now talking about.

"I've got to get out of here" he spoke to no one.

"Got to get out of here" he repeated as he fumbled through a stack of scattered papers on some desk near his bed.

"Got to write"

Joe Simpson wrote whenever he was disturbed. Since now he was traumatized, he knew he had a lot to write. The writing he made while coping with any sort of anything was in the form of bizarre stories. He would let his mind wander and conjure up and create anything it so desired. He grabbed a stack of white paper and 2 blue pens.

Out the door he flew, somewhat franticly. He was putting on his jacket while trudging down the street when he decided where he'd go.

After several moments of running, Joe was in the fields at the side of Mission Avenue- a place away from the devastation. There was no one there, and this contented him. He set himself against the trunk of a tall tree, surveyed the surroundings for a moment then delved into writing. After 45 minutes, Joe put the paper and pen down and looked up in surprise, like he didn't remember where he was. He saw the road with no traffic. He saw the deadish tall grass, the green trees and a few birds which flew through the cloudless blue skies.

The paper he'd been scribbling on was white, now marked up in blue.

"Why am I writing? - What" he paused.

"What am I writing about some fairy tale world for? There's been a damn earthquake. People are dead and I'm- "he stopped and just stared into the surroundings.

Hey there reader, I am walking along the destroyed mall of Santa Cruz. All these policemen, all this tape. You see friend, they can't stop me. I can do anything. I've got form now and more. You know the nice woman Susan whose sweaty arms I just left. She solidified the last part of me I needed. You dear reader need not read anymore and I am still here. If you'd stopped earlier it'd be different, but ah, thank you!

And that bloke Joe, he is the one who really helped me. He read my voice, conjured me from the potential to the solid- even tried to destroy me. But do you know reader that if you didn't read this then Joe couldn't have done anything. He wouldn't have existed either. You are our true makers.

I am not going to bother these good police men. I shall stand here by the red tape and watch them try to make heads or tails of this mess I've made. You, of course, know I caused all this.

Look over there. A vigil for some woman in the coffee shop rubble.

You know what I really want to do? I'd like to be in one of those grey army helicopters that keep flying here. Yes! I shall go do this. Read on, my fine reader. Read on- or don't. See if I care.

Bolovo Pete turned from where he stood and walked away from the street. He walked toward where the grey helicopters took off and landed. As he did, one of those machines came chopping over the horizon. Bolovo Pete walked in his leather jacket, with cigarette in mouth.

As he walked by Joe Simpson's house he stopped, looked up, then turned sharply from his course and walked in. Joe Simpson was in the meadow writing and no one else was there. Bolovo Pete glanced around then strolled into Joe's room and began picking up and reading his stories which formed a pile on the desk.

"Ah, this is useful!"

He settled himself with casual ease onto Joe's bed and continued reading and smoking. He even walked into the kitchen and grabbed a beer and some cheese, then made his way back into the bedroom and onto the bed.

"What lovely fears."

He bit into the cheese, continuing to read.

"Oh, this is lovely! I can use this!!! I'm feeling more powerful every day. So many fears."

He sipped the beer then heard the front door as it opened.

"Company- WHO IS IT?" Bolovo Pete yelled from his comfortable position on the bed.

Ed Saker, one of Joe's good friends and housemates, was surprised by the unusual voice and the tone it carried. He walked down the hall and into Joe's room where he saw the reclining figure of Bolovo Pete on Joe's bed, blowing smoke out his nose, and gazing with excitement at some paper.

"Where's Joe?" asked Ed.

"Oh, Joe, I don't know. I just strolled in. I'm a good friend of his. You must be Ed Saker."

"Yes." Ed was surprised. "Who are you?"

"Bolovo Pete"

Ed looked closely at this person lounging before him, while Bolovo Pete continued to read as if Ed were some ignorable insect.

"Oh, Bolovo Pete you say?!"

Ed walked away into his own room where he sat down. He was confused. Joe had told them about some guy stepping out of the page he had been reading. They had thought he was nuts. Maybe he'd drank too much coffee or beer. He had been frantic when he told them. He was obsessed. The morning before last- the day of the earthquake- he had shown them a box with a mirror in the bottom.

"This will take care of Bolovo Pete" he had said. They began to really worry about Joe then and planned to talk to him. Of course the earthquake changed this plan as it changed so many others- leaving practically no plan in Santa Cruz whole.

Now there was this guy, who called himself Bolovo Pete and who had an attitude of complete carelessness, lounging in Joe's room. Ed wondered if it was a joke, or was some misunderstanding. He walked back into Joe's room.

"Excuse me, how do you know Joe? I mean who are you?"

"I am Bolovo Pete! What more need I say"

"Who are you? Where are you from? How do you know Joe?"

"I am Bolovo Pete. Leave me- go away!"

"Listen man, you just walked into my house; I don't know who you are; you helped yourself to my beer; you're eating our food and we don't know who the hell you are!"

"For the last time, bug off. I'm Bolovo Pete. Leave and close the door behind you."

Ed was dumbfounded.

"Who the fuck are you! Get the hell out of my house!"

Bolovo Pete lay there reading never bothering to even look up.

"Listen to me! Get the hell out of here!" yelled Ed as he yanked the story out of Bolovo Pete's hands. "You've got some attitude. If you're a friend of Joe's I'll be surprised."

Bolovo Pete sat still, staring at the place where the paper had been. He then looked up into Ed's eyes.

"I am gonna murder you"

Ed drew back.

"Just get the hell out of here."

Bolovo Pete rolled off the bed onto his feet and then stepped toward Ed, who was backing away. Ed stopped backing up and faced him:

"Get lost you bum- you can't kill me, get the hell out of my house."

Bolovo Pete walked until he was face to face, practically body to body, with Ed.

"Oh yeah? I caused this." He motioned his hand to indicate the whole of Santa Cruz. "I am your worst fears- yes, hit me. I feel it. Hit me!"

Ed swung with might at the figure. With a dull thud, his fist struck the gut.

"Harder. Hit me harder" Bolovo Pete smiled. Ed swung harder striking him in the stomach, in the face, everywhere he could imagine, but nothing phased Bolovo Pete. It didn't seem to affect him at all.

"You see! I am invincible. You've even more to fear" said Bolovo Pete who stood there. Ed backed off and ran to the other room toward the telephone.

"You think the police are gonna come here now? There's no police. They're all out there." Again Bolovo Pete motioned his right hand to indicate the town of Santa Cruz with its brick heaps and taped off streets,

Ed ran out the door. Bolovo Pete laughed, then made his way back to Joe's bed where he set himself up as he'd been before and continued to read from where he'd left off.

I woke up like so many times in the past. Even in my transformed state the fear had become real. Just a body- just a sex thing. I was treated like an object again by some creature I didn't know. When it lay there at night I felt a longing to have it.

I licked its neck and it shed its clothes and became free like me. We intertwined, became so close, so colorful, and so expanding. There was satisfaction till sleep set in.

I fell asleep and woke to it handing me shackles. It tried to make me take clothes from its hands, then said something about "Bolovo Deep" and "fears" and walked off.

I watched the creature walk with assurance and confidence like it had no fears. In its arms I had felt secure and comfortable. It was the kind of lover I'd always thought I wanted. Tenderness, intimacy gentleness and holding. I felt safe and at peace. Here was what I wanted I had thought.

The morning sun woke my body and the creature was out of my arms standing looking at me- I felt a pang as I saw it looked at me now as if I were carnage. My naked, sweaty, muddy body it looked at, then tried to give me clothes to cover it. The creature was distant and removed, and I felt the familiar void, the familiar longing and pain.

It talked at me: "Bolovo Deep", "fears". It must be called "Bolovo Deep". It must know my fears I thought while I watched it walk away and while I felt a desire to chase and kill it. But fear stole my whole being, and stopped my limbs from moving in any direction.

The "Bolovo Deep" walked away like nothing could stop it which seemed the truth to me. I didn't feel I could. The fear creature "Bolovo Deep" intrigued me though. I had to get it out of my life. I was still transformed, and I knew the "Bolovo Deep" must be dealt with. I knew somehow that my life would become everything I ever wanted it to be if I did face this mighty creature.

Ed Saker, in a state of the numb, walked about damaged streets looking to his left and right, seeing policemen and seeing firemen who were obviously busy and to stressed to give time to him.

Bolovo Pete was the center. His image shone in Ed's head. The terror he'd felt was all he could think about- something uncommon.

"He was going to kill me- but he was a bluff all along- Joe said he stepped out of a table or was it onto a table- I could see him stepping onto a table- I can't believe it."

He wanted to go and deal the being a good slaughter but his whole self yelled for help. Finding nothing of power which promised to vanquish the enemy, he walked on spinning within.

"My punches did nothing. Nothing- but nothing. He didn't even feel- flinch- just smiling. How? What is he?"

He stared at his hands while his legs carried his torso through hordes of gaping people, their mouths open and fingers pointing to Santa Cruz's rearrangements. Ed Saker was beyond earthquake thinking. His mind was nearing Mars- his thoughts landing routinely on the face of Bolovo Pete.

It must now be said while Ed walked in stupor, Joe was creating creatures in his mind by the fields of Mission Avenue, and Susan Pikkins, also in the fields, was passed out from exhaustion. For after Bolovo Pete left her side, she ran on all fours, in a dynamic frenzy full of rage and anger and grunts which she made like a sow.

Cuts, scratches, blood, and filth were on her. When her arm fell into a gopher's hole, she collapsed, thanks to gravity, and lay there, body down and arm in, face in grass and sky overhead. Not moving, just staring, she looked at nothing and drifted away from everything.

In this nothingness she saw everness and in the everness she saw stories which can more properly be called images, but hallucinations will do for explanation. Unmanifest possibilities of popular thought bubbled in her brain and questioning notions took control and set out on the course of explaining the world in ways it had never been explained before:

"Greeks had molecule machines which could change water into rocks or any other things like that. The machines, given to them by buzzards, helped in the establishment of art. Art really was water, but it became rock when the molecule machine was turned on." So thought Susan Pikkins as she lay there amidst the scene of swaying nature.

"The machine" she continued, her mind running over every type of western fact officer that stood, uniformed and all, to stop her. They usually had their hands out and the golden whistle to their lips. But Susan saw them not and sped over their mental forms continuing to blaze the wallpaper of accepted logic.

The western fact officers, as administrators of the emperor Loe Jic and his decrees, wore their blue suits and could be found everywhere, usually standing bored and alone blocking roads where thoughts were not to travel. These untraveled roads, obviously full of dust and age-set debris, were now the alleys for Susan's mind. She raced down them seeing things not even high ranked fact officers had seen. Her wheels set ablaze dust showers and her being took any path it wanted in the ancient golden city of Original Thought.

"The machine-" she continued as she read the road signs along the alleys in Original Thought and as she lay motionless "runs on space and there's tons of that around. Pulley in space, making water into art, creating planets from the voids in the sky. Trojans had oil derricks and they had crude barrels but didn't know what to do with them, while over the hill in Egypt were those special facts which are no more.

"They were called supertoads and all the kings' horses and all the kings men liked to eat toads- they - the toads liked being eaten very much. And around this area were mechanical cars which were a plenty for all, but one of the real ones were dead- that's why religions took them to arms and petted and rubbed them with specialness and attention.

"And then there were Yees from long ago and they were in legend known by the Phoenicians and Babylonians..."

At this point I'd like to clarify everything as narrator. Bolovo Pete you have met and heard that he's the manifestation of everyone's fears. Susan Pikkins, as beautiful as can be imagined, thought she was a pig. Joe Simpson was the writer haunted by Bolovo Pete. And Ed Saker was one of Joe's housemates. You shall meet the others in a moment.

Now we have the logic emperor, Loe Jic- one of the last characters you need worry about. He becomes part of the cast. As you can imagine- being one of his subjects yourself- he was lord of the thinking realm. His logic officers guarded corridors and they made sure one did not enter them, for should this happen it was the realm of voidless comprehension that was entered, where minds could drive for lifetimes and never get out.

One must remember this even today and avoid the alleys they still guard. But even if you forget, the logic officers are there to stop you. But as Susan Pikkins in the story has gone through the edge- many of these usually bored logic officers have been killed by her speeding, out of control mind. She has gone where one is not allowed to go. The logic emperor was obviously quite aware of what happened since this was a rare occurrence. One did not often go into the boarded-off city of Original Thought.

He gave the order: "Catch Susan Pikkins and bring her back to my domain." The problem was Susan Pikkins was inside the city of Original Thought- where he and his logic officers had no maps since no maps could exist there. She was running wild and they were trying to find her.

The log emperor and his officers and Susan Pikkin's mind were in a different world than the one Joe and Ed and even Bolovo Pete dwelled in at this time. Susan's hands and legs still sat motionless in the fields of Mission Avenue while her mind spread age old dust in the gold paved city and while the logic emperor and his officers prepared to explore the unknown city.

The only thing you should store in your mind at this point is the word "YEE". More shall be said, but now…

I'm just here reading from my space of being. Yes, real being, my fine creators. Real being, just like the truth and your mind and eyes.

Joe's writing intrigues me- I like it, for you see and must understand, your fears are art. Such wonders of creation, amazing masses of work. The hours- the time- quality of your life you put into them- look at this. Pages and pages of fears. And you too. Yours are great. I love them. And Susan Pikkin's- the quality of hers are monumental- a Mozart- I've never seen anyone make it into that metropolitan cesspool- Original Thought. Mozart himself was quite wonderful- a great friend- a great friend.

Yes- of course, what's going on I know. All these things I know. It amuses me. That your life is reading this does too.

What am I doing here? You ask me. Why? Rather, what are you doing here? Business of what sort have you here to pry into other peoples' lives? Why are you so nosey? It is- do you find me nosing into your life? Perhaps I should- It wasn't me- it was you who began prying- "Who's this Bolovo Pete?", "What is he?" Now you want to know.

By the way, another point, - Are you??? Wouldn't that be interesting! Yes!! Anyway, if you are or aren't, I'm still leaving. I'm sick of this room. I'm bored of these stories. Don't get me wrong; art still they are- but that which is too familiar is too familiar- a good saying, one which should be remembered. Remember this. Goodbye reader.

Bolovo Pete threw the stories from his hands, yanked on his leather jacket and strolled through the door into the living room. As he did this Susan Pikkins, whom hours ago was with him, zoomed over fractions and definitive prototypes.

The logic emperor had chosen his squad of top officers and set out in a mighty formation- like some hoplite army- to dissect the city's streets and find the woman. They had unboarded the alley on DESCARTES AVE and with special helmets and armor on, they proceeded into the city which he referred to as "void of thought". Of course the emperor and each of his officers had a rope attached to his or her back so being pulled back into the realm of sanity was again possible. It was even reasoned these ropes should be of metal so one deluded by the surroundings could not, in a state of madness, cut the cord and wander about with no strings attached. Emperor and his 300 specials entered the city in 6 groups with 50 in each. The 6 squadrons took 3 routes; Emperor staying with the middle one.

Something should be known. In thought-dimension no speech need be made. Emperor was well aware what each officer did, as he's aware of the same with you. His job was to find Susan.

At this moment Bolovo Pete exited Joe Simpson's house. After standing on the road a moment, he walked toward where the helicopters were landing and taking off. At this moment also, Ed Saker at the top of the hill which held the university, was appealing to his other housemates who had spent the earthquake night on campus.

"You've got to believe me! Like Joe said, that guy Bolovo Pete is real!" said Ed with pure sincerity which his friends Carl Gil, Heaney Mart, and Less Moodsy could see.

"You think I'm joking, man, but this guy was in Joe's room just lounging there-"

He told them what happened.

"And oh- he knew my name when I first came in-"

"What'd he look like?" asked Carl

"Tall, long dark hair; he has this leather jacket- it's like he's not afraid of anything. I split. Ran out of there so fast- Boom out the door. Took off- didn't know what to do."

"You did the right thing" said Less. "Do you think he's still there?"

"Probably! We can't do anything to him though. He's invincible-"

"No one's invincible. There's a way. He's just really strong," suggested Heaney.

"Now wait," spoke Less, "is he the type of person to use a gun?"

"You aren't hearing me!!! He doesn't need a gun. I don't think a gun would kill him-"

"Oh! A gun would kill him!! What are you talking about-a gun wouldn't kill him; a gun kills anyone," spurted Less.

"He's not anyone!! There's no one that could be hit like that and feel nothing."

"Let's see your hands," said Carl.

"Let me see if I've got this straight," inquired Less, standing tall and looking at his friend full in the eyes.

"This guy who calls himself Bolovo Pete, who Joe was all freaked out about, was kicking it on Joe's bed at our house and he refused to leave and said he'd murder you, and you hit him and it did absolutely nothing-"

"Then I ran away and it was like he just laughed and wasn't worried of anything."

"He sounds evil," inserted Heaney.

"Let's find him," added Carl.

"No, wait. We'll get the police on him. That's what they're for. To do our dirty work," suggested Less.

"That's no good. He challenged me to call the police. It's like he's aware of it all and not afraid of anything."

"He'll be afraid of the police! With their clubs! BAM! Come with us Mr. Bolovo Pete," chimed Less.

"You're not hearing me at all!! He's not human!"

"We could call the cops and tell them he's a Martian-"started Heaney.

"-You're not hearing me!! He's not human!!!! Remember Joe saying he stepped out of a table?"

"Yeah, but he was joking," Less replied.

"No. He was serious. He's been strange," said Heaney.

"He's been really out of it. I thought he was losing it- but what you're saying is like what he's been saying. The other night he was rambling on about the guy Bolovo Pete; you remember it Heaney," added Carl.

"He was. I thought he was joking but he was acting serious," verified Heaney Mart.

"Oh, and Bolovo Pete was also talking like he caused the earthquake!!! Which doesn't make sense- but maybe it does. He kept gesturing with his hands saying, "I caused this"," added Ed.

"Some loony," ventured Less.

"He was serious"

"Didn't Joe say no one could see this Bolovo Pete guy but him?" inquired Heaney.

"Yeah- he did. Why could you see him?" chimed in Carl Gil.

"I don't know!!" said Ed.

"Maybe it had something to do with the earthquake?" suggested Less.

"Huh?"

"Maybe the earthquake made him visible," Less clarified.

"I think more like he made the earthquake," said Ed

"Drop that. No one can make an earthquake." declared Carl.

"He maybe could. He's like an evil god!!" Then Ed Saker's mood switched to one of pure desperation. It was as if he would die if they didn't comply. It was as if he were in some trance of fear. He was not acting normally in the least.

"He's got to be stopped- will you guys help me get him? He's got to be stopped!! He caused the earthquake. He's afraid of nothing. I don't know what to do- He needs to be stopped I know this. He's dangerous. I've never felt so much fear in my life. It was like facing a loaded gun. One that might fire in your face."

"What are you saying we should do?" asked Less.

"Find him!! He's either at the house or somewhere else."

"Well, that makes sense. But what are we gonna do once we find him if he's this powerful being you say he is?"

"I don't know. We've got to find him though. We've got to find him! Help me find him, you guys. Help me- We've got to find him!" Ed was even more frantic.

"I'll come," said Carl.

"I'm there," said Heaney.

"Well, let's go," said Less.

The four threw on their small backpacks and left the university library. On the way to the street each picked up a large stick and some of them put some rocks- also of the larger proportion- in their backpacks.

They realized the bus was no longer running due to the earthquake so they walked down the big hill, toward town in caravan formation to find the being Bolovo Pete. As a matter of interest, Bolovo Pete was no longer at their house; instead he was very casually strolling along Laurel Street on his way to the helicopters.

Logic emperor, upset at searching for the runaway ex-subject of his, was annoyed that his logic officers kept blundering, coming to situations which were not supposed to exist. They were smacking into circumstances which were impossible, according to every rule or hypothesis of logic. As an example, one officer was saying he could no longer search because his feet were too good. Another said he had found two Susan Pikkins. Another said he <u>was</u> Susan Pikkins and that they should keep searching for him.

"What to do?" flashed in the mind of uncorrupt logic until finally he figured he'd have to find her himself, using only his own mind. Relying on his officers for no consistent help, he set out to do such.

Susan Pikkin's body lay motionless on the soil which sustained the fields of Mission Avenue, while her mind rounded a bend in the forgotten city's corridors and headed straight toward the emperor. He heard the noisy motion, looked up and saw this unbelievable spectacle. She was roaring along the ancient road. Streams of age old debris rose seven feet from her trail then glistened down like snow through a rainbow.

Her speed was tremendous. The mass of her mentalness approached infinity. Collision appeared inevitable. All statistical levels of thought used by the logic emperor warned him of the danger he was in, thus he wisely braced himself for impact.

Susan tore toward him. He held his arms out until POW!!!!!

There was trampling. Susan, trampler. Royal highness logic emperor supreme, tramplee.

He lifted himself from the alley, hollered to some officers, and set forth to capture the woman.

Because of his undisputed authority in a dimension where most people lived, the logic emperor was used to being obeyed. Lack of recognition was something completely new to him. Needless to say it greatly disturbed his peace of mind, and his whole being ached with wonderment.

Could such a person really exist and not recognize him at all- even when he went so far out of his way as to personally rescue her? It had been eons since there was anywhere else besides his domain, and he couldn't' remember what it had been like.

"Had it been like this?" he wondered.

In his new, shaken mind set, he decided he needed to gather advice from the top officials of his kingdom. Able to do this mentally he sat down in the dusty lane and met with the big wigs of LOEJIC.

You know, reader, I am not stupid- no- not stupid at all. I know what's going on. I know who's after me- with their sticks and some rocks. They think they can hurt me. Oh- it is wonderful! Wonderful to see such fear in action. Amazing. The mirror was smart, but rocks?! I think General Cergo tried the same thing with me- but oh- so long ago was that.

They are near Mission now. Close to me, but I will make them wait. Yes! Wait they must.

And Susan I know where she is too. The logic Emperor. And you!! I know exactly where you are.

Joe Simpson's most interesting now. He's walking about the fields rather near Susan- I say no more. I am ready to ride this helicopter. There is something so nice about helicopters. They just twirl upward.

Twirl, twirl, twirl. I love the way they twirl. And all those police people so worried. Like they think something's important- something's so tragic. The earth shook. Big deal! And if they thought I caused it, that'd be great too. They won't believe me. Poor Joe Simpson. He's fascinating. Almost as good as Susan.

The quality of fear ceases to amaze me. What I'd really like to see is one of them explode me with a tank, then for me to tap hem on the shoulder. Oh, this fear would be exquisite. Perhaps top. Maybe I'll take a helicopter to Susan.

No, I am not in the mood. It is something more satisfying I feel like doing. Yes, yes. Paying Susan another visit. A visit for Susan. That'd be better. But no helicopter- no- no helicopter.

Bolovo Pete pulled a cigarette from his black, beat jacket of leather, lit it, watched another helicopter begin to twirl away into the blue sky. He exhaled smoke, stood in peaceful silence.

There were police lining up in a row on the high school's baseball field, which was also serving the city as the helicopter launch-pad. With a calmness serene, he turned his stare at the mass of adults and kids gathered watching the huge machine take off and watching what the foreign police were going to do. He smiled as the police officer, in war gear, marched off in chaos. The gathered group of observers disassembled; some followed the police; others going back to their nearby homes or tasks. Bolovo Pete looked on till all were gone, then turned aside and walked. He headed toward Mission Avenue.

Now logic emperor had found a sure way to pull Susan Pikkins into his world again. It was fool-proof and thoroughly consistent with his character. He sent his chief officers, while he sat, waiting for her guaranteed capture. The officers, clad in the blue uniforms and whistles, moved out. The logic emperor remained motionless on the wavering plain.

"A despicable place," he thought, "but I could see it tamed," he said while looking around at the undefined. Once he realized it'd be impossible to pave the alleyways of Original Thought, he thought further about the plan which guaranteed to capture Susan. Officers had marched in with sticky nets which dangled across the alleys. Sooner or later they'd run into her, and since she had no logic reverence in the head, though seeing the net, she would not stop and capture would be eminent.

Where was Ed Saker? He was with his posse of friends searching for Bolovo Pete and Joe Simpson. The latter they hadn't seen since before the earthquake which shook the senses and buildings and roads and bridges. Where was Joe Simpson? He was wandering the fields of Mission Avenue this while. Where was Susan Pikkins? She lay motionless in body and in mental flight from Emperor's officers of logic supreme.

Joe, who had disgusted that part of himself which criticizes with ease, resorted to picking grass, rolling it into balls and throwing them at nearby trees. Trees in this area of California- it must be noted- grew large and green and had no way to move from projectiles aimed at them. They were relatively defenseless. Another well-deserved point, which now shall be made, is that Santa Cruz, being a beach town on California's coast, was full of what could be best called beauty, manifest in grass, flowers, moist earth and pretty insects.

The butterfly variety of insect fluttered about at this time. Some neared Susan Pikkin's prostrate form. Others in the same vicinity came upon meandering Joe Simpson. It is reasonable and accurate to now assume the two protagonists were within distance of meeting one another. They had never met, but meeting looked inevitable, since Joe Simpson's feet carried him toward Susan's motionless body.

I'm not sure what I was doing lying naked and filthy on the grass; I remember only vagueness; some figure in blue with medals all over its chest; soldiers with whistles; nets; yelling; dust; freedom; running through walls, over buildings, into surfaces. I think these figure things were furious at me. It was like I'd angered them by being who I was- still it's vague what happened.

I do remember waking from that realm, seeing this different figure looming over me. It looked saddened and dull. I stared into its eyes. There was pain. It was heavied by living, like trucks were sitting on its head. I was entranced by its suffering and wanted to kick it at the same time I wanted to love it. Why should another creature get to feel pain like me? It wasn't fair. I wanted to attack for sake of territorial claim. It was on my turf and had no right to be. The eyes of the figure had no right to hold that look in them. It was mine- and only mine.

I jumped and its leg I bit as hard as I possibly could. Coolness and warmth- skin and blood; screaming and jumping, staring at me in further alarm like I was something unseen until then, the creature pulled away but my teeth held its leg firm. Words were flung as I clung on.

This creature would suffer for suffering. I wouldn't let it get away. I held it. I was still a pig.

Ed Saker with those friends arrived at the street corner of Mission and Laurel. They debated whether to go straight to their house on the mall or to get more friends to help in the search. At this same time Santa Cruz was still in hysterics over the town's forced alteration. Electric power was out. The sun was about to set which of course meant the world would get dark. Lines were at stores. 7-11 had locked its doors. Water and batteries were in top demand. With cameras and wide eyed people wandered everywhere. Fires- all of which had been put out by now- still gave ashes to the Pacific air. Traffic, left in anarchy, was majestic. The streets were ruled by mountain bikes; police were everywhere; volunteers even.

Carl Gil, pointing to a twisted house, said,

"Let's forget about Bolovo Pete. Look at this! We need to check out the damage."

The others disagreed. They'd been convinced by Ed's tone that Bolovo Pete was a mystery worth discovering.

"While we're looking for him we'll get to see all the damage," said Heaney. "This way we have a purpose."

"We should get baseball bats," said Less sharing his idea.

"Why don't we pillage. There're endless stores and this is prime shopping time!!"

They walked down Laurel Street and past the helicopter field which Bolovo Pete was walking away from. He smiled as they passed, though no one was in seeing distance. He couldn't see them. They couldn't see him; nonetheless, he did smile, then walked toward laurel Street. He headed toward the intersection they had just left- the corner of Mission and Laurel.

After standing on the corner a moment, musing over the lines of cars and the people everywhere animated in different modes of excitement, he turned and walked along Mission toward the fields where Susan was about to bite Joe Simpson.

It yanked and yelled as my mouth held firmly. What it was saying I didn't know till the word "Bolovo Deep" came out. I desired to kill. Either the creature before me or anything else, but most of all the Bolovo Deep thing which had slept on my body the night.

My teeth sunk in harder and I felt pain outside of me. An equilibrium- first, it didn't feel right to bite the creature in my mouth, but then it did. I was fluctuating. "Bolovo Deep" it yelled again as if in inquiry. I was a happy pig and felt threat.

This creature held by my teeth, it had no right to threaten me. Bolovo Deep was my fear. No one else's. My head began spinning. Breasts and blood, a leg, I saw. For a moment I was a mud covered naked woman, until I squealed, regaining pigness and safety.

"Woman" it yelled tugging against me. "Woman". My spinning head saw breasts, fingers; tasted blood. The creature was feet away holding its leg, terror-eyes gazing at me with its mouth floating open. Corn to eat was in my pig's mouth, or was it human flesh? A woman, a pig, a pig-woman, a pig. The creature stared at me as fluctuations of form shook my being. Its eyes, the only piercing constant. Earthquake? -Pigquake- loose date- fear cake- colors. Smelling colors, green circles, yellow square, orange reds, blue lines, spinning, spilling, spitting, brown, pink, white mud, grass, grain, eyes, horns, skin, pulsation- inside. Caged in colors.

I was caged in colors. ;. The creature looked on. "Woman," "Woman", "Bolovo Deep".

What had happened in that golden city was as the emperor of logic, clad in his blue uniform, had predicted. While he sat wondering whether it was possible to map the back alleys of the city, adding new territories to his kingdom, his officers wearing sense-proof masks protecting them from the outside chaos, carried nets across the alleys. It took many hours, but ultimately Susan Pikkins came running full force down a lane. The sticky net lay in front of her, but this changed nothing. With ferocity she raced on, entering the middle of the net and attempting to continue on as if it weren't there. She began to drag the logic officers on either end until they aligned the controls inside their face masks which in turn allowed them to simultaneously resist her speed.

Eight officers pulling in the opposite direction slowed her down, and she would have continued to drag them like cans from a wedding car if not for the royal supreme emperor of logic who, at this time, appeared on the scene.

The being Susan Pikkins, moving at a slow speed, in the midst of a sticky net, pulling eight logic officers, was trackable. She was no longer logicless. She had a tail now; and this tail the emperor caught up to, ran alongside and ultimately lassoed with a steel cable.

Not only his eight logic officers holding the net, but also Susan Pikkins herself was contained in the cable's grasp. The other end- of course- was pulled so that nine minutes later the bundle of beings emerged from the other side of the broken boarded wall- the same wall she had run through earlier. Sirens and authorities were everywhere. Being in the logic realm meant being completely containable. They carried her to the headquarters and waited for the emperor to return across the threshold.

Less and Carl, Ed and Heaney arrived at their house, found no one, then decided to go back toward the university. Why? Because Ed was frantic. He wanted to find Bolovo Pete. Since they didn't see him around the mall, he figured the "demon" would be found away from the mall.

"That's ridiculous thinking," said Carl. But Ed was convinced and pushed his view. No one argued further.

"You lead," spoke Less. The others followed. From their house they grabbed flashlights and rope. Rope was Ed's idea.

"This is so we can tie him- if he's tie able."

Walking away from the house, they stared at disastrous stuff: At the red brick rubble. At the darkening sky. At officers and volunteer officers, and firemen, and people everywhere. Everywhere. At buildings sitting sideways. At broken windows, broken merchandise, broken mannequins and trees and cars. A jumbled normality facing their eyes and senses, like a library after some truck's driven through it. Isle racks over and books everywhere, Santa Cruz, with her funky shops and streets, and people, and animals, and things had been shook, and all the things in Santa Cruz took the ride; their forms shaken and little pieces created.

Ed, Less, Carl and Heaney saw the pieces. Everywhere were pieces, and the setting sun made them dark. Lightless streets, lines of cars, mountainbikes, exploring crowds, curious eyes, smoke of smoldering fires, rumors, death, fear of dying, voids of fear, celebrating, sex, all this was about.

Tears, hugs, hand holding, sadness, hopefulness, phone lines clogging. This all began to effect Carl, Less, Heaney and even Ed's emotions. No longer was it solely a search for Bolovo Pete, it was now, also, a search for the center. What had begun as fun and sticking together became sticking together and a quest for stability. They were about to head towards the fields of Mission Avenue.

The corner of Laurel and Mission was stuffed with traffic. Even as the sky darkened into a hazy orangeness, cars pushed their way along the naked roadways.

Ed, Less, Carl and Heaney stared at the mess of what had been a sturdy store. Entertainment and chaos. They waved to friends along the way, and one of these friends joined them on their journey. Her name was Mira. They had told her the story. She decided to come along. Who wouldn't?

Ed Saker was intense. Beads of fear illuminated the roundness of his eyeballs. He turned in circles while they walked, as if searching for something.

At this moment, Joe Simpson, less than half mile away from this posse, was hopping about with Susan attached to his leg. He was amazed at her nakedness and earthen filth. It was not a beast, but a beautiful woman biting him. Part of his insides filled with expansion. His eyes, after rubbing, still saw beauty and his mind pondered the possibility of everything.

"What is going on?" was obviously his thought.

The pain was immense until he pulled free from her teeth. The two then stared at each other with a small distance between.

"What the hell did you-," he said mixed with anguish and astonishment. It made no sense; this spectacle in this environment.

"What are you doing, woman?" Susan just stared at him.

"Is it the earthquake?"

All four of her limbs were on the earth and her naked body was painted with mud. She looked athletic and rugged. But she said nothing, just stared at him.

Joe looked deeper into her eyes and there it was. Something he'd never seen before, yet knew so well. Hysterical fear of what he couldn't define. Somehow he knew it was related to his own fear. With stunned caution and utter frozen shock on his face and body posture, he slowly asked:

"Bolovo Pete!?"

She lunged, with teeth. As he jumped backwards out of her painful reach, he realized and said, "You have seen him."

And as a matter of interest, Bolovo Pete was a step away from being in view of those two, then of a sudden, he was visible to them and they to him.

Joe was stammering those words at Susan. She was staring at Joe deciding whether to attack again. Lo0gic emperor was on the throne curiously watching his ex-problem Susan, who had recently returned into his world's domain (i.e. LOEJIC) from a point of invisibility, he watched as all was going well.

She obeyed his laws. That she was emotionally disturbed was not his problem. Only that she use logic. With ease and renewed confidence in his competent supremacy he leaned back in the throne and smiled a logical smile.

"Hello my friends," called Bolovo Pete to Joe and Susan. Their eyes darted with ferocity. 4 eyeballs. 4 cannons of fear.

"You're looking stunning Susan! Hello Joe! I'm here to introduce you."

Both Joe and Susan stood in utter silence. Their mouths open showing petrified terror. Their bodies unable to move an inch.

"Cat's got your tongues. But you do look good that way. Come. Come. Don't mind me. Continue your discussion," spoke Bolovo Pete while he strolled up to them. His attitude held no doubt. He walked like a knife through butter cake.

"Ah yes Susan! You should attack me. Bite me hard. I'd like that in fact! Well? Have you no feet?"

He looked at her with a confident smile. The leather jacket was on. His arms held positions of ease at the body's side.

"Well?" he repeated.

Susan lunged at him, running on all fours at first then standing onto two legs for the first time in days.

Bolovo Pete moved not an inch. No muscle flinched. It was as if nothing at all were happening.

As Susan's teeth sunk into the flesh, there was no scream. No pain. No blood. It was like she'd locked her mouth onto a radial car tire.

Frustration immense. She bit and bit and bit and bit and hit and hit and punched and kicked. Nothing did anything. Bolovo Pete stood smiling continually. He seemed to be enjoying himself.

"Oh, you can do better than this."

She hit harder, bit harder, kicked harder. Still no pain. The smile persisted. Joe wanted to kill him too. He wanted to attack. With what? His eyes searched the surroundings. Rocks, sticks. Then, something changed in his head.

Something puzzled him. There was a solution. He stood dumbfounded and obviously disturbed with decision. What to do?

"Yes Joe!" began Bolovo Pete, while Susan continued to hit and kick and sock him with tremendous strength. He spoke around her body as if it were of no significance. This obviously made her fight more fiercely.

"Why don't you pick up the rock by the tree? It looks sturdy enough. My skull should collapse under the weight."

Joe heard him, of course, but the urge to follow the advice was countered by something powerful inside which was quite in active focus. What was it? The solution. Yes. The solution? He resisted an urge to clobber Bolovo Pete with the rock. It was such a strong urge, but something inside was stronger.

It was at this exact moment that the posse, Ed, Carl, Heaney, Less and Mira, saw Joe and Bolovo Pete and Susan Pikkins in the field. They saw Susan attacking. They saw Joe standing and they ran as fast as legs could carry them to join the assault.

This bunch gathers to attack. But you must agree. I am complete when you see me. I am as real as you make me. Yes. You reader, too, are my savior, my creator, my destroyer, but you know this. You play with my fate dear reader like the fish in the water- like the- you know though.

Control my destiny! Shall I cause another quake? Shall I cause the earth to tremble and more fear- yes fear- to roam the surface? To roam your life? Shall I blow your mind?

And what of Susan beating me now? Hit her? Shake her? Throw her to the ground? What would you have me do? Be?

They shall all attack. But they can do what? They are who? Who are you?

Ah- the beauty of might. The beauty of fight. To attack what you're afraid of. To strike the unknown- which threatens. Beauty. Again I say beauty. Like an exploding star, like a crumbling mountain, like a slicing iceberg- but what have I to say to you, reader, who creates all I see? You, reader, who can make me stronger and stronger.

You know? - Well, they attack me! Why don't you? Throw the page down! Curse me! Fear me- fuel me!

Reader, know who I am! Know what I am! Know all of me! Know what I say! Read, dear reader! Yes! Reader, read. Give me the strength I need. Read with your fear! Like a broken record, smash me!!

Bolovo Pete, their target, they charged ferociously. Less Moodsy smacked him on the legs with his stick. But, of course, nothing resulted. Ed Saker in his frenzy, tore and yanked at the body. It was no human what he touched; more like a tree of metal. His weight against the figure did nothing. His fists did nothing. Carl's hair yanking, Mira's punches, Susan's biting did nothing. In fact no ones assault did anything damaging.

There was a problem with having enough room for all six to attack him at the same time. Each took their punches and kicks, while he smiled and stood. With each punch he smiled more and more.

Joe stood away from the commotion, transfixed, while Less broke his big stick over Bolovo Pete's head, while Susan smashed her fists into his face, while Heaney strove to knock him down, while Carl focused on kicking him to the ground, while Mira pushed him from behind.

The group was in a panic. They grew angrier- more intense- more violent, yet no satisfaction was awarded their thrusts to destroy. Their thrusts to kill- to conquer.

The smile on Bolovo Pete's face reached illumination.

"Yes! Kill me!!!!"

The sun shone. Bugs crawled. Planets spun. Helicopters chopped. And six humans beat and beat on the figure which would not fall. Each hit he withstood with grace and serenity complete- with peace and ease. With some type of bliss.

I was biting the first creature. I was feeling its pain in my mouth. It pulled away and looked with fear. What was it looking for in me?

I turned toward a sound from the right and saw the walking manifestation of fear itself. It was him! The Bolovo Deep.

As fast as I could move I was at him- to kill. The killing I was sure of. I was going to kill him. When my teeth sunk into its neck- in the Bolovo Deep- it felt no pain. More the urge to kill- to kill. The more I attacked made no difference. It was fearless, senseless. My heart ached.

I was on two feet, a woman biting a creature. A pig biting a creature. A woman, a pig. From the distance I saw figures, then there were strangers all about attacking the Bolovo Deep. I felt company-familiarity-belonging. Was I a pig? What was I? Who was this I attacked? Why did I attack it?

One moment it felt safe to bite, then - of a sudden- it felt ridiculous. What was happening to me? The safety, the peace- my pigness- was fading. My identity was losing- What was I doing? - Why was I doing? - Where was I doing? Who were these strangers? These people? These creatures? This creature I had attacked just earlier?

This Bolovo Deep- he was a demon- fear itself.

I hit I, bit it and no feeling came from it. The creature I had been biting had felt pain. I had seen a similarity to me in it.

The Bolovo Deep and I had nothing in common, except fear. Yes. Fear. It drew my fear. With fear I bit hard to kill. Kill it!!

The first creature- the man? - stood back, watched, did nothing. Why didn't it attack? I attacked. Why did a smile shine from the Bolovo Deep? It shone beyond me- through me. To it, I was not anything. The other creatures- men and a woman? - Why did they attack? - Why? - What were they attacking for? What was I doing? What was I to do? -Should do? What was going on?

The six, in a frenzy, beat on Bolovo Pete, and Joe watched confused. The confusion then dismissed itself and understanding took stage.

"Stop!!!" he yelled. The solution was clear.

"He's not real!!! He's our creation!"

The others surrounding and hitting Bolovo Pete gave no attention to Joe's words. He flapped his arms and jumped up and down:

"Leave him alone! There's nothing to him. He doesn't exist!!! You are creating something that's not real!!!- stop nurturing him!!! Stop hitting him!!!! He's your own fears!!!"

Less Moodsy and Heaney Mart paused and looked at the others and at Bolovo Pete who stood in front of them smiling.

"What the hell are you talking about?" yelled Less. "He's as real as-"

"-I'm as real as any of you! That's right!! And I'm now going to kill you all!!" yelled Bolovo Pete as he turned his body so his face and eyes stared straight into Less Moodsy.

"I will start with you."

Less raised his fists to strike. Joe yelled with shrillness.

"No! That's what he wants you to do! Why the hell do you think he turns to you?" But Bolovo Pete loudly cut him off, and with a fierce glance proclaimed:

"Joe Simpson! You are too much of a coward to fight me. You are afraid!"

"See!!- He's all bluff! Just tries to scare me into fighting. Never hits back. He can't. All words- He'll just scare you. That's all he can do."

At this point Mira paused from hitting Bolovo Pete and Carl followed suit, doing the same. Only Ed Saker and Susan Pikkins continued to attack- and that they did well, though it was obviously of no harm to their attackee.

"He must be destroyed!!" yelled Ed as he backed away from the target, then ran and kicked it with full force. Carl and Heaney grabbed and held him.

"Stop! What if this does strengthen him?"

"I don't care! I will kill him!!" screamed Ed Saker.

The demon, amused, watched them yelling at one another while Susan continued beating on him.

"Well, Mr. Bolovo Pete, why don't you recognize the only one strengthening you?" Joe said referring to the naked woman giving all her effort to destroy Bolovo Pete.

"You see, my friends, I am going to kill you! That is why I've lead all of you into this barren meadow. She's the only one putting up resistance. You all have accepted your fate. I caused the earthquake, destroyed your city, and am now going to destroy your lives."

Joe flapped his arms, looked up at the sky, which was darkening quickly, and yelled:

"Bullshit!! You caused no earthquake. You hurt none. You can't hurt anyone. You can only make us hurt ourselves. You lie!!!"

Bolovo Pete's face darkened, and he walked straight for Joe with what appeared to be the intentions to assault.

Carl, Less, Heaney, Ed, and Mira approached Bolovo Pete. A few of them began picking up rocks.

"What the hell are you doing!!!? Don't feed him," screamed Joe. "He can't do anything to me!"

The figure of Fear, himself, arrived face to face with Joe, who didn't move at all. Reaching into his leather coat, Bolovo Pete pulled out a knife.

"Are you sure this is what you want?" he asked with calm confidence.

Susan withdrew and watched in awe. The others gathered in suspense.

Suddenly, Ed Saker's eyes lit up. He looked at Joe and smiled.

"Go ahead," Joe responded, calmly.

Bolovo Pete raised the knife high and prepared to strike.

"No, wait!!!" screamed Ed.

Bolovo Pete's head turned to face Ed, and as usual there was a smile on it.

Ed jumped up and down and sideways and in circles.

"Kill all of us! We'll line up. Kill us all! Please Mr. scary Bolovo, hurt us, kill us, maim us!!! We'll cooperate!!"

Ed Saker was smiling. Joe Simpson smiling. The others weren't. What was going on? Confusion?-

There was a pause- a breaking- swelling- floating pause. After which Mira, Carl, Heaney and Less joined in:

"Kill me too!"

"Please kill me too."

"Kill me too?"

"No, kill me."

The five pranced around Bolovo Pete while Joe stood at ease next to him.

"I'll kill you all then!" retorted Bolovo Pete.

Susan was the only one not dancing or smiling. She didn't run though. In awed silence she watched.

Joe sat down on the ground, like some soccer player at half-time. He stared up into Bolovo Pete's eyes.

"What do you want here?"

The others stopped dancing. No one appeared afraid except Susan. It was curiosity which now motivated their silence.

"My friends, I want nothing! You do not understand who I am and that I can do anything. I could kill you if I wanted-"

"Then kill us! Right now! Let's see it. We're patiently waiting."

"Hit me at least!" begged Ed.

"We see right through you."

Bolovo Pete looked dazed, yet calm. He shook his head as if he'd forgotten money for an important event, then he turned and walked away from them.

"You know I thought the earthquake forged him," added Less to Joe.

"That's an idea. Hey is that true? The earthquake create you?" yelled Joe to the demon who headed straight toward Susan.

She froze. Fear was battling her.

"Ignore him!" yelled Heaney.

"You're stronger than him!" yelled Mira.

"Hello Susan-"But Bolovo Pete could say no more. She was on the ground sobbing. She huddled into a fetal-ball and cried and cried. He sat next to her, placing his hand on her naked shoulder.

"It's ok Susan. I'm here. Everything's gonna be all right."

She continued to cry. He continued to sit there, his hand on her shoulder. The others stood in awe wondering what might happen. No one dared interfere.

"You know how I feel about you Susan."

Then, it happened!!- Susan sat up and stared into Fear's eyes. She wiped her of their tears, stood up and looked at the sitting figure. Slowly- ever so slowly- a genuine smile crept onto her face.

I was face to face with him. The others had laughed at him. They weren't afraid. The first creature who I'd attacked before, his eyes shone. The others caught it. Their eyes shone. It was me and the Bolovo Deep.

It walked toward me, and I fell and cried. The fear- longing- hopelessness was everywhere. What to do? I cried.

It put its hands on my body, which caused satisfaction of a degree, but there was something empty and unsatisfying about it.

It lied to me with more words. I knew it was lying.

It was lying! Totally lying!! That was it!! It <u>was</u> a lie. I realized it <u>was</u> a lie, and I could tell.

I knew it was a lie and felt no fear.

I knew my being a pig was a lie. I saw my legs. My filthy legs. And my breasts and my hair. I saw tears and soil.

Yes. I could tell it was a lie.

I could tell the difference. There was no truth to it.

I stood and stared into the Bolovo Deep. There was nothing there. They were empty eyes. Like mirrors, or glass marbles. They were eyes which could only lie!!!

I felt reborn- great- empowered, and I walked away feeling completely free and alive for the first time in my life!

Thus ended Bolovo Pete's special assignment to Santa Cruz, California. His mission done, there was no reason to stay.

Zap- he was gone.

Zap- he was home, in his own world. A world of fields and flowers and suns. The land where Yees lived. Where spotted dragons lived. Where chompers chomped and beakplants swayed in a cool spring breeze.

His own house was here. And he was very excited to be back. With speed he made his way through the fields of beakplants and past some Yees. There were no chompers about.

He came to his door and walked in. On the table was a note:

"WELCOME HOME MY DEAR ONE. HOPE ALL WENT WELL ON THE JOB. I'LL BE BACK SOMEDAY SOON. I LOVE YOU."

Bolovo Pete smiled, then made his way to one of the two big chairs which faced a large amount of glass that looked out into the meadow full of Yees and beakplants and a few spotted dragons.

He sat down, sighed contently, and looked out the window.

www.ingramcontent.com/pod-product-compliance
Lightning Source LLC
Chambersburg PA
CBHW071342130626
46556CB00005B/1985